Chasing
Dream

Backyard ∩ Horses

Dandi Daley Mackall

author of the bestselling Winnie the Horse Gentler series

Tyndale House Publishers, Inc.

Carol Stream, Illinois

Library of Congress Cataloging-in-Publication Data

Mackall, Dandi Daley.
  Chasing Dream / Dandi Daley Mackall.
    p. cm. – (Backyard horses)
  Summary: Even though she has spent the week doing selfish things, nine-year-old Ellie asks God for help when her beloved horse becomes sick.
  ISBN 978-1-4143-3918-4 (sc)
  [1. Horses–Fiction. 2. Christian life–Fiction.] I. Title.
PZ7.M1905Ch 2012
  [Fic]–dc23
  [pcc]   2011040858

Printed in the United States of America

18	17	16	15	14	13
7	6	5	4	3	2

To Katy Mackall, my first editor on all things animal

Backyard horses are the opposite of show horses. They don't have registration papers to prove they're purebred, and they might never win a trophy or ribbon at a horse show. Backyard horses aren't boarded in stables. You can find them in pastures or in backyards. They may be farm horses, fun horses, or simply friends. Backyard horses are often plain and ordinary on the outside . . . but frequently beautiful on the inside.

✹ ✹ ✹

The Lord said to Samuel, "Don't judge by his appearance or height, for I have rejected him. The Lord doesn't see things the way you see them. People judge by outward appearance, but the Lord looks at the heart."

1 Samuel 16:7

1

Wild West

It's the most important race in the old Wild West. Ellie James and her speedy horse, Dream, step up to the starting line. Next to her, Cowboy Colt lopes in on Bullet, the famed cow horse. These two trusty steeds join fifty other horses. They're all itching for a chance to ride for the Pony Express. The winner of this here Wild West race will earn a spot on the Pony Express, America's new mail delivery system. Horses will deliver the mail across the United

States (since mail trucks and airplanes haven't been invented yet).

BANG!

The sheriff shoots his pistol. The horses are off and running!

Bullet and Dream take an early lead. It looks like they don't plan to give it up, either. Off they go—through the desert, into the mountains, across the wide-open prairies. Folks cheer as hooves thunder down Main Street. Riders gallop past the old saloon, past the sheriff's office, past the church with the white steeple.

Dream and Bullet are neck and neck as they cross the finish line. It's a tie!

"Hurray for Colt and Bullet!" the crowd shouts. "Hurray for Dream and Ellie!"

"Ellie?"

The Wild West fades back into my imagination. The dusty prairie becomes the tile floor of my

2

classroom in Hamilton, Missouri. Cheers are swallowed up by the stern voice of my fourth-grade teacher, Miss Hernandez. She looks surprisingly like one of the cheering prairie women from the Wild West.

"Ellie, answer me, please. Are you or aren't you ready for it?" My teacher tugs on her ponytail, which is one of the best things about her. Her ponytail, not the tugging. Tugging means she's losing patience with me because she caught me daydreaming again.

"Uh," I begin. "Hmmm. Am I ready or not? Good question." I'm stalling for time because all is not lost. I'm looking for my best buddy, Colt Stevens.

Lucky for me, my teacher has walked over to my desk. That means Colt is behind her. One of the best things about Colt Stevens is that he took up sign language when I did. We learned it so we could talk to my little brother, Ethan. But sign language also comes in handy for helping each other out of trouble in the classroom.

I could sign *What?* to Colt, but Miss Hernandez knows a little sign language herself. So I just raise my eyebrows at my buddy.

Colt grins, then finger-spells *r-e-c-e-s-s*.

Recess? Cool. "You bet, Miss Hernandez!" I answer. "I am *so* ready!"

My teacher looks confused. She doesn't have old wrinkles like my parents do. But her forehead squeezes wrinkles into it anyway. "Really, Ellie? Well, good for you. I'll expect to see great improvement from you, then."

Great improvement? At recess?

"Totally," I say. Only my stomach is getting funky.

Colt is laughing now.

"I guess you've been studying, Ellie," Miss

Hernandez says. "Because we all know that those fourth-grade math proficiency tests can be tough if we don't study, study, study."

Colt Stevens! Our teacher did not ask if I'm ready for *recess*. She asked if I'm ready for the state math tests. That answer is a big, fat no. I'd like to sign something mean to Colt for tricking me. Only his back is turned. I can see his shoulders bouncing up and down like he's riding Bullet at a trot. He thinks this is so funny.

I gaze out our classroom window until the green grass turns into the dust of the Wild West again. Then I back things up:

Bullet and Dream are neck and neck coming down the stretch. They gallop lightning-fast toward the finish line. It sure looks like it's going to be a tie . . . until Cowboy Colt starts laughing. His shoulders shake. He topples to

the side. And boom! Colt falls off his horse,
landing in a soft mud puddle. Poor Colt is left
behind in a cloud of dust as Ellie and Dream
cross the Pony Express finish line.
Hurray for Ellie and Dream! The winners!

Miss Hernandez hands out more math home-work. Our teacher is in the middle of another pep talk, explaining to the class how important those tests are to us and the state of Missouri and the whole entire United States of America when the speaker system comes on.

"Would somebody please find Ellie James?"

I blink a few times to make sure I haven't imagined this. I haven't. I'm in my classroom staring at the speaker like everybody else.

Slowly, kids turn and stare at me. Rashawn and Cassie look more worried than a pair of spooked horses.

From the speaker, a squeal, or maybe a scream, is followed by a shuffling of feet. There's a crash like a chair is being knocked over. Then I hear the voice of Principal Dwayne Fishpaw shouting, "*Now!* Tell Ellie to come right this minute! There's a horse in the library!"

2

The Library

"Go, Ellie!" Miss Hernandez opens the door. "That's you!" she shouts like I might not have noticed our principal screaming my name over the classroom speaker.

I'm halfway out of the room when Miss Hernandez changes her mind and calls me back. "Ellie, wait! Don't forget your math assignments."

Colt grabs my books and papers and shoves them into my backpack. Then he runs up to the doorway. "I'll take your stuff with me. And I'll walk

Ethan home after baseball practice. Good luck with Fishpaw."

I think I thank him. But I'm not sure. I'm too worried about what I'm going to find waiting for me in the library.

I race down the hall. A kid can get yelled at for running in the hallway. But I figure compared to what they'll do to a kid whose horse is in the library, running in the hall is nothing.

Slowing to a fast walk, I spin around the corner. Two more steps and I'm at the Hamilton Elementary School library door.

I send up a quick prayer without words because I don't know what to say. Then I step inside.

The first thing I see is our principal. He's standing on a library table by the fairy tale section. Principal Fishpaw is the size of two regular dads. The tufts of hair on his head are sticking straight up. He's wearing a suit and tie. His socks and sandals are in full view because he's lifting his pant legs like water is rising.

I start to say something to him, but then I spot my brother, Ethan. His class must be having library period. Second graders are scattered around under library tables and chairs. They're giggling like kindergartners. Ethan is the tallest kid in his class and the only one not hiding under a table. He's sitting board-straight in his chair, and he's circling his fist on his chest. It's the sign for *sorry*.

Definitely not a good sign.

I hear a nicker from somewhere behind me.

Every other time I've heard that soft rumbling sound, it has made me happy. A nicker is a horse's sign of friendship. It has always been my favorite greeting.

Only not now.

I turn, pretty sure about what I'll see. "Dream! What are you doing here?"

My sweet, beautiful, black-and-white pinto is standing in the corner of the library, right in front of the animal section.

There is a very good chance that I'm imagining this whole entire day.

I walk up to my horse. I touch the ear-shaped spot on her chest. No other horse on earth has a spot like this one. Yep. Definitely my mare.

Dream nickers again and nuzzles me.

One of the second-grade girls says, "Aw." The rest giggle.

Principal Fishpaw, still standing on the table, yells, "Ellie James, get that horse out of my school! Now!"

"Yes, sir. I-I-I don't know how she got here. She can't get out of my backyard. My dad made a super great fence and—"

"Your dad?" Principal Fishpaw roars.

I glance at Ethan. We both know Principal

Fishpaw and my dad have history. Dad used to go to school here when he was a kid. He spent a lot of time in the principal's office.

Ethan looks at me and shrugs his shoulders.

I take hold of Dream's halter and start to lead her out.

"Stop!" Principal Fishpaw says. "Ellie, on second thought, stay right where you are. Don't let that horse move a whisker!" He looks around the room until his gaze settles on the potted green plants by the window. "Mrs. Ford?"

Mrs. Ford, the librarian, stands up from behind the plants. Her blonde hair looks like she's been riding a racehorse in the wind. "Y-yes, Principal Fishpaw?" Her voice makes her sound like a second grader.

"Mrs. Ford, will you please come out from behind that plant and take these children back to their classroom?"

"Of course, Principal Fishpaw." She starts shooing kids out from under tables. Two boys are huddled in one corner. They're rolled up like a ball. But they unroll when Mrs. Ford comes for them.

"Time to go!" she pleads. "The bell will ring any minute. Have to get your things together, children."

Finally the library is empty except for Principal Fishpaw and me. And Dream, of course.

Principal Fishpaw frowns at me. "Well?"

I'm not sure what he wants. First he said to go. Then he said to stop. And it's not my fault Dream scared Principal Fishpaw onto a library table. *I* didn't bring Dream to school . . . although I do sometimes imagine riding my horse to school. I picture ducking low and letting Dream climb the main steps to my classroom. She'd have her own desk, a big one next to mine.

"Ellie?" Mr. Fishpaw is probably waiting for me to say something.

"Y-yes, Principal Fishpaw? I-I'll go home now, sir . . . with my horse."

"That's all you have to say?" he bellows.

"Um. I'm really, really sorry?"

He scowls at me like this is the wrong answer too. "This better not happen again, Ellie. You tell Leonard—your father—that he'd better fix that fence for good! There is no excuse for shoddy work, be it in the classroom or out."

Principal Fishpaw is the only person in the world who calls my dad Leonard. Mom calls him Lenny. Or honey. Or dear.

"Go!" Principal Fishpaw stands so tall on the library table that he bumps his head. "Ouch!" He crouches and points toward the door. "Get that horse out of here!"

The bell rings just as Dream and I step into

the hall. Kids pour out of their classrooms. When they see my horse, they run up and try to pet her.

I'm afraid Dream will shy away from kids or get spooked by so much noise. But she doesn't. She lets them pet her, even though sometimes people aren't gentle enough. And sometimes they're not careful around sensitive spots, like her ears and flanks.

Ellie's Dream is the best horse in the whole world.

"What's that smell? I can't believe they let that nag in here." Larissa Richland blocks my exit outside.

A couple of girls in my class gather around Larissa like she's queen of Hamilton Elementary. She shakes her short red hair, and her perfect curls bounce. "Girls," Larissa says to her royal court, "this is why you never want to get a backyard horse."

Larissa believes any horse that's kept in the backyard, instead of a stable, isn't fancy enough to be a *real* horse. She would never own a horse if her parents couldn't trace it back to famous horse ancestors. She'd have no problem selling her own horse if it quit winning prizes for her in horse shows.

I'm pretty sure Larissa's horse has never even seen her backyard. When she calls Dream a backyard horse, she thinks it's a huge insult.

But I love having a backyard horse. Backyard horses make the best friends. Plus, it's great having a friend live so close. If Larissa wants to see her horse, she has to make her parents drive her an hour away, to the elite K. C. Stables. I just have to open my window.

Dream and I manage to edge past the fourth-grade royalty and head for home.

"Dream, you know I love hanging out with you. But you can't come to school."

I listen to the musical clip-clop, clip-clop of my horse's hooves. We're right between spring and summer, and every tree is showing off bright-green leaves. Hints of clover and newly grown wheat come with the breeze. Morning glories peek from the sides of houses. But the best smell is horse—*my* horse.

I try to shake the image of Larissa and her snooty friends sticking up their noses at Dream. The whole school will be talking about my horse getting into the library.

I put my head against Dream's neck as we turn onto my street. Bullet, Colt's gelding, whinnies to us from Colt's backyard pasture.

"Dream," I murmur, "I wish everybody at school could see you the way I do. You're the best horse in town. If only I could prove it. . . ."

I stop.

Dream stops with me.

"Dream, that's it! I am going to prove to the whole school that you're the best horse in town!"

18

3

A Plan

Before I reach the backyard, I have a plan. A super terrific plan. A plan that will prove once and for all how wonderful my horse is.

Question: How can I prove Dream is great?

Answer: By letting people see her *do* something great.

Like win a race.

I know my horse is fast. She's way faster than Larissa and Ashley and the other kids would believe. They need to see Dream's speed with their own eyes.

So I am going to have a race.

I lead Dream around the side of the house to the backyard. My dad and I did a great job building a home for my horse on short notice. When I got Dream at the cat rescue farm, where my mom volunteers, we didn't have much time to make a spot for her. I'd always imagined having a horse of my own. I prayed every night for a horse. I just hadn't imagined *this* horse. Dream came as a surprise for all of us. But my whole family pitched in, and we put a fence around our whole backyard and built a lean-to—a three-sided wooden building where Dream can go when she feels like it.

"Okay, Dream. Let's figure out how you got out of this yard. Did I leave the gate unlatched?" I'm pretty sure I didn't. Dad put on a bar latch that clicks into place when you shut the gate, and I'm always careful to check it.

I take a look at the latch. It's still in place. And

the gate's closed. "Weird." I open the gate, and Dream and I walk in. Like always, I shut the gate behind me.

"Maybe Dad spotted the gate open and came out to close it. Or maybe the fence is down somewhere."

I turn Dream loose in the yard. Our backyard is more like a small pasture. Our house is the last one on this side of Hamilton. Hamilton, Missouri, is a small town. Dad says it hasn't grown a lick since he was a kid. You could fit 254 Hamiltons inside Kansas City, Missouri. I know this because my friend Cassie put it in a report she did for class.

I walk the fence to see if there are any holes Dream could have squeezed through. There are only three sides of wooden fencing. That's because the fourth side is our house.

Everything looks good. No holes. No posts down. Everything is perfect.

I check the lean-to, but everything seems normal there, too. Our lean-to is bigger than three stalls at K. C. Stables. So far we've left it open on one end. But we'll probably build a fourth wall and put in a door before winter. Then we'll have our own little barn—a backyard barn.

I turn to face my horse. She's already grazing as if going to the school library were part of her regular routine. Pinto Cat has taken her usual spot on Dream's back. The calico came with Dream from the cat farm. Pinto Cat comes and goes as she pleases. But not Dream. Not usually, anyway.

"You're a mystery, Dream. I don't suppose you're going to tell me how you got out of this yard, are you?"

She swishes her tail, but she's not telling.

"I know *you* won't give away the secret, Pinto Cat. So there's no use asking you. Guess I'll have to ask Dad."

I give my horse a hug around the neck, holding on long enough for one more whiff of horse. "You're the best," I whisper. "And pretty soon everybody in Hamilton will know it."

I find my dad hunched over his laptop at the dining room table. Papers are scattered from one end of the table to the other. "Hey, Dad!"

He looks at me, and all at once his face gets swallowed up in his smile. The best thing about my dad is that he's always happy to see me. My mom thinks Dad is the most handsome man "on God's green earth." She claims that nobody can hold a candle to Lenny James.

I love my dad and wouldn't trade him for any other dad. But in the looks department, I think he's kind of average. Short like me. Not too fat, not too skinny.

"Ellie! Thank goodness you're here. I need help with this ad campaign for Harvey's Hardware."

Dad works for the Jingle Bells Ad Agency. Whenever he needs rhyming jingles, he comes to me.

"Sure, Dad. But first I've got to ask you something. Did you close the gate this morning?"

"What gate?"

"Dream's gate."

"No. Was I supposed to?"

"So you never saw the gate open after I left for school?"

Dad takes his fingers off the keyboard. "Ellie, what's this about?"

I tell Dad about Dream showing up at school and me getting called to the library. Only I leave out the part about Principal Fishpaw standing on the library table.

"How do you think your horse got out?" Dad asks.

Before I can answer, the front door opens and

in walks Ethan. He's carrying his baseball and bat, and he looks excited about something.

So does Munch, who thunders down the stairs to greet him. And I do mean thunders. Our mutt won't stop growing. He already weighs way more than I do. Ethan braces himself for Munch's lunge. The dog pounces, putting both paws on my brother's shoulders. I don't know how Ethan stays on his feet.

Even our lazy cat, Squash, waddles out from under the table to greet Ethan.

What am I—chopped liver?

Ethan is already signing when he reaches Dad and me. *I hit one over the fence*, Ethan signs. *And Paul was pitching*.

Paul is the starting pitcher on Ethan's team, even though Ethan is a better pitcher.

Dad and I congratulate Ethan. We do this with words and with sign language, spoken at the same time. That's how we always talk around our house.

"Wait until your mother hears this," Dad says.

Ethan turns to me and signs, *Principal Fishpaw didn't give you a note for Dad, did he?*

Dad almost falls out of his chair. "What? Why? What do you mean, Ethan?" Then he looks at me. "Ellie?"

So I tell Dad the rest of the story. About my principal shouting from the top of the library table and telling me to get Dad to fix the fence.

Dad looks like a little kid who got caught cheating on a test and has to answer for it in the principal's office. "He called me Leonard, didn't he?" Dad says.

I nod. "But don't worry. Tomorrow I'll tell Principal Fishpaw that your fence wasn't the problem after all. It's a great fence, Dad. And a super gate, with a foolproof latch."

Ethan interrupts my little pep talk. *So how DID Dream get out?*

4

Sorry

Ethan has a way of getting to the heart of things. How *did* my horse get out of our yard?

I still can't answer that one. And I'm tired of trying to figure it out. All I want to do is forget that Dream was in the library and get on with my plan.

The race. I need a name for it. And contestants. I know Colt will be up for a good race. And Rashawn and Cassie. I can invite Ashley and some of the kids from our horsemanship group too.

"You don't think I should call Principal Fishpaw, do you?" Dad asks.

"What? Principal Fishpaw?" I have so moved on that for a second I think Dad wants to invite my principal to our horse race.

Bad idea, Ethan signs.

"Ethan's right, Dad. Don't give that library incident another thought. *I'm* not going to."

But I can tell my dad is starting to get nervous about the idea of going to the principal's office again. This calls for a change of subject. A change of worries. I try to guide Dad back to his original worry. "Tell me about the new hardware store campaign. What do you need rhymed?"

Ethan says he's got homework and excuses himself. He takes off for his room, followed by Munch and Squash.

Dad scoops together a bunch of the papers strewn over the table. "It's a tough account, Ellie. Harvey's Hardware has always been one of our hardest-to-please clients. That's why my new boss gave it to me. I get the feeling she'd love to see me fail."

Dad's new boss is Moira Stevens, Colt's mother. She works for Jingle Bells too, and she was just promoted to vice president. That job could have been my dad's. Then he would have been *her* boss. But Dad turned down the promotion because it meant a lot of travel. He didn't like the idea of being away from us.

Colt's mom took the job instead, and she's gone a lot now. Since she and Colt's dad are in the process of getting a divorce, poor Colt gets left with a different babysitter—or "house sitter," as Colt calls them—every time his mom takes off on a business trip. A couple of times he's had to stay with us because Mrs. Stevens couldn't get anyone else. I didn't mind at all. It made it that much easier for Colt and me to ride our horses together before school.

Dad fills me in on Harvey's Hardware. "Why couldn't Harvey be running a campaign to sell nails or whatnot?" Dad complains. "Even I can think of things that rhyme with *nail*. Like *pail*. Or *mail*."

"How about *sale*?" I chime in. "*Come to the big nail sale!* That would have been too easy." I flash Dad a grin. "There's always *bale*, you know. Like bales of hay?" Dad and I have a running joke about how I always try to rhyme his campaigns with horse words.

This time he ignores the joke. That tells me he's really worried about this campaign.

He sighs. "Ellie, how am I ever going to come up with words that rhyme with *barrel*?"

"It will be okay, Dad. We'll think of something. Not to worry." Only nothing comes to me right off. I force myself to concentrate. "Can't rhyme *barrel* with *barrel*, or we could bring in barrel racing."

No reaction.

"You know? Like horses running barrel races? Galloping in and out of barrels, weaving around big barrels?" Still nothing. "Like Colt's horse, Bullet, racing . . ." I give up.

"Don't suppose the campaign will run over Christmas?" I ask. "We could use *carol*, like a Christmas carol."

"I wish I did have until Christmas," Dad says. "I need to have this done by Saturday. That's when Vice President Stevens is making me do my presentation for the hardware people. I have three days to be brilliant."

I feel bad for Dad. I want to help him out. Really I do. But most of my brain is already used up trying to figure out how to organize the horse race. "Um . . . *Darryl*? Nah. That won't work. *Feral*? Like part wild, as in feral cats?"

Just as I say it, Mom bursts into the room like the Fourth of July. She's wearing a long red-white-

and-blue-striped dress and red tennis shoes. She plops down the rainbow-colored bag she calls a purse and exclaims, "Did somebody just say 'feral cats'? Or are these old ears of mine running amok?" She kisses the top of Dad's head and then my head and slides into the chair next to Dad. Even sitting down, Mom is a head taller than he is.

"Hey, Bev," Dad says. "Your ears are perfectly fine. And the prettiest pair of ears I've ever seen, by the way. Ellie was trying to help me with this campaign Moira Stevens threw at me. We're trying to rhyme *barrel*."

"Moira Stevens." Mom lets out a snort-sigh that could rival Dream's. She swivels around to face me. My mom has clear blue eyes and short black hair. Her hair is the only not-colorful thing about her. "As for you, Ellie James, I have a bone to pick with you. Where in Alphabet City were you this afternoon?"

Then I remember. I was supposed to go help Mom at the cat farm after school. "I forgot. I'm sorry, Mom."

"Sorry won't fry the bacon or bring it home. Whoo-whee! Did we need you today! Cats running all over the cat farm, and Mary Louise and I were about as helpful as hogs on ice without ice skates. We were counting on you to provide some quiet time and comfort to cats that needed it. We had three that required some one-on-one time in quarantine today, and I had to fill in for you."

"I'm really sorry," I tell Mom. I mean it, too. I know she's been extra busy at the cat farm since she took on a new responsibility there. She's the feline foster care head volunteer, which means it's her job to find temporary homes for stray cats.

The best thing about my mom is that she doesn't just say, "Aw, too bad" when she feels sorry for an animal. She jumps in and does something to make things better. Most nights she has to make dozens of phone calls to try to place a single cat.

"I'll make it up to the cats," I promise. "Maybe I can help you with your new job, Mom. Like I could make some of your phone calls."

Thinking about phone calls reminds me that I need to start calling my friends about the race. I want to have our horse race as soon as possible. Why should I wait any longer to show everybody what Dream can do?

I get up from the table and head for my bedroom. I don't have a cell yet, but at least I have a phone in my room.

"Ellie, where are you going?" Dad asks, panic in his voice. "What about my rhymes?"

"I won't forget, Dad. I'll make a list of rhymes for you. Okay?"

He looks relieved. "Great. Thanks, honey. You always come through for me."

I spend the rest of the night on the phone. By the time Mom peeks in to tell me it's bedtime, I've called just about everybody in our whole class. And it's a go. The first annual Fourth-Grade Horse Race will take place after school on Friday at the Hamilton fairgrounds.

As I drift off to sleep, I remember to say my prayers. I ask God to bless everybody. Then I tell God I'm sorry about forgetting the quarantined cats. And right before I conk out, I remember I didn't study for my math proficiencies. So I toss that one in too.

5

Ready

Larissa Richland is waiting for me when I walk into our classroom the next morning. In all the years we've known each other, Larissa has never waited for me. No way can this be good.

"There you are, Ellie James!" she shouts.

"Yep. Every Monday through Friday," I answer.

I move past Larissa toward my desk. But I keep one eye on her. Granny used to say, "You can put glitter on a glue stick, but it's still a glue stick." I don't know what that means. And I can't ask my grandmother because she died when I was little.

But Mom quotes her a lot. And she says this glue stick saying is for when people try to act fancier than they are.

Larissa follows me to my desk. "So why didn't you call me?"

"Was I supposed to call you?" I ask. But I think I know what she's talking about.

"Duh. The race?" Larissa glares down at me. If I'm as short as a second grader, she's as tall as a sixth grader. "You called everybody else about your little race. But you didn't call me. Why not, Ellie? Could it be because you know Custer's Darling Delight and I would win?"

I stand as tall as I can. "No. I didn't call you because your number is unlisted." The Richlands are the only people in town who won't put their number in the Caldwell County phone book.

A bit of the punch leaks out of Larissa. But she snaps back, "I have a cell, you know."

"I know," I say, slipping into my seat. "And when exactly did you give *me* your number?" Last night I realized all I'd have to do was ask Cassie for Larissa's number. I guess I wasn't all that anxious to call her. But not for the reason she thinks. Larissa's three-gaited American saddle horse would be the favorite in a horse show but not in a race. I figured I get enough Larissa at school.

"Well, just so you know, Custer's Darling Delight and I will be at your dumb race," Larissa shouts. She says it loud and standing up, even though the school bell already rang and everybody else is sitting down. "And we're going to win!"

"Larissa?"

"What?" Larissa spits out the word at top volume, then spins around to see who said her name.

Miss Hernandez gives her ponytail a tug and says calmly, "Larissa Richland, take your seat. You and I will have a talk about this during recess."

"But that's not fair! It was Ellie's fault. She–!"

"Take your seat, Larissa," Miss Hernandez says. "Now."

Our whole class gets super quiet. This is the first time in five years of school, counting kindergarten, that Larissa Richland has gotten into trouble with a teacher.

Today is off to a good start.

★ ★ ★

At lunch all anybody can talk about is the big race. At least at my table. Rashawn and Cassie are my two best friends (besides Colt), and they both have backyard horses.

"This is such a great idea, Ellie," Rashawn says. "Dusty isn't very fast. But I still think a race will be so cool. I'm going to braid Dusty's mane. It's really grown out over the spring."

"Perfect!" I tell her. I love Dusty. She's a big dappled farm horse, as sweet as they come.

"That will be awesome!" Cassie agrees. "Her braids can match yours."

Rashawn's mother usually braids Rashawn's hair in neat rows of tiny braids. I'd give anything to be able to do that. My hair won't even stay put in one braid.

"Is it okay if I ride bareback?" Rashawn asks.

Dusty is over seventeen hands high. It's like the eighth wonder of the world that Rashawn can mount that horse bareback.

"Of course you can ride bareback," I answer. "You can ride any way you want."

"You know," Cassie begins, "I think Misty might be fast." She stares at the table, then grins at us, her blue eyes wide. "I'm not saying that to brag or anything. I'm not even sure if my horse *is* fast. I've never let him run all out. It's just that he's always wanting to go faster."

My friend would never brag. Cassandra Bennet, "Cassie," is one of the prettiest girls in our class. Her hair is blonde, and no matter how it's cut, it does what it's supposed to. She's as popular as Larissa and Ashley. But it's like she doesn't even know it. Or care.

"I'll bet you're right, Cassie," I say. "I've seen Misty run. He's got short legs, but they move like lightning. It'll be fun to see what he can do." I take the last bite of my peanut butter sandwich. That's what my mom makes for my lunch. If I want something else, I have to buy it.

Rashawn is leaning on her hand, elbow on the table, and staring at me. "Ellie, what made you decide to have a horse race anyway?"

I think about how I want to say this.

Rashawn presses me for an answer. "Couldn't

have anything to do with Dream being in the library yesterday, could it?"

"Maybe." I get a flashback of Dream and me leaving the school and Larissa and her friends laughing at us.

Then I get another picture of when I first saw my pinto on school grounds. She wasn't mine then. She looked scraggly and skinny. She tore around the school yard, dodging the animal control people. The entire school was laughing at her.

"I guess I want to show everybody that my horse isn't some kind of joke. I want people to see how wonderful Dream—"

"Aw, isn't this cute?" Larissa interrupts sarcastically. She turns to Cassie. "Are you bringing Phony Pony to watch the big race tomorrow?"

"My pony's name is Misty," Cassie answers. "And *Misty* and I will be racing on Friday."

"How cute is that!" Larissa exclaims. She

turns to Rashawn. "Don't tell me you're bringing Musty too."

Rashawn glares at Larissa but keeps her cool. "*Dusty* and I will be there. Thanks so much for asking."

Larissa turns her red head in my direction. "Wait. Ellie, I thought this was going to be a race . . . not a tractor pull."

Every year at the fair, there's a tractor-pulling event. Giant horses, like Clydesdales, compete to see how far they can pull big farm machinery. Larissa's crack is a direct slam on Rashawn's horse. And I won't stand for it.

"What's up with you, Larissa? Are you so worried about the competition that you have to make fun of everybody else's horse? Why don't you save it for the race?"

"Oh, don't worry about that, Ellie," she says. "I'll have plenty left for the race."

6

Get Set

After school, Colt and I go riding together. We walk the horses down our road until gravel turns to dirt. Then we trot. I still haven't gotten a saddle, so I'm riding bareback. At horsemanship practice, Mr. Harper, Ashley's dad, lets me borrow any of the saddles Ashley's not using. Sometimes I ride Western, sometimes English. I'm not sure how I'm going to ride in the big race.

I glance at Bullet. When Colt got his horse, you really had to use your imagination to see the cow horse underneath all that fat. But Bullet's muscles are taking shape again.

"If you ask me, Colt, I'd say our horses are looking good. Dream has gained so much weight, I'll have to start cutting back on her Omolene pretty soon. And Bullet is really slimming down."

"I can't wait for Bullet to be in tip-top shape," Colt admits. He frowns, and he's quiet for a second. "It was strange—yesterday I found the lid off of the can where I store his oats. I could have sworn he'd broken in and eaten half of the oats in there. But when I looked for him, he was still out in the pasture. There's no way he could have gotten into the bin from out there."

Colt is bouncing a little too much in the saddle. But his riding skills get better every day we take the horses out. "I guess Bullet will lose the rest of the weight in his own time. Until he does, though,

I'm afraid to make him gallop hard. I don't want him having a heart attack."

"I know. You're doing the right thing." We turn left at the Penney farm. J. C. Penney grew up in Hamilton. Dad says my great-great-grandpa went to school with "Jimmy Cash." But eventually he left Hamilton and opened all those department stores, and the farm was sold off to someone else.

"I wish I could all out compete in that race of yours, but I can't. Bullet and I will be in it but just for fun. When my horse gets in shape, I'll demand a rematch."

"You got it." I feel bad for Colt. He's so competitive that he can't stand losing at anything. I hadn't thought about Bullet not being able to run. I was too busy thinking about showing off Dream's speed. "How about I make it up to you?"

Colt squints down at me. I think he gets taller every day. And tanner—not that I'm noticing. It's only May, and already Colt has an August suntan. "How are you going to do that?"

"Barrel racing. I know Bullet can't run barrels at a gallop yet. But he could start at a trot or maybe a canter. I've got the barrels from Dad's Harvey's Hardware campaign. They're not the kind you'd have in an official barrel race. But they'd work for practice."

"That's not a bad idea," Colt says. He leans down and strokes Bullet's muscled shoulder.

"Plus, I could help you with the rules and everything. I've read so many books on barrel racing and cutting horses. What do you say?"

"Great! Thanks, Ellie." He urges Bullet into a gentle lope.

I lean the slightest bit forward, and Dream eases into a canter. We keep pace with Bullet and Colt until we're past the Penney farm. Dirt crunches under our horses' hooves. Dust clouds puff up behind us. We make our own breeze on a windless afternoon while geese honk from a crooked V overhead. And everything in me tells God, "Thank You."

As soon as we get back, Colt wants to start setting up barrels in my backyard. But I need to practice for the race. So Dream and I head to the fairgrounds by ourselves.

When I ride up to the fairgrounds, I'm surprised to see Ashley Harper already in the arena. The Harpers have their own stable and their own horse arena. That's where we usually have horsemanship practice. Mr. Harper owns more prizewinning show horses than one rider can handle. Ashley rides Cindy Lou, a beautiful three-gaited mare, in saddle horse competitions. If she's entering a jumper division class, she rides a bay gelding called Hancock's Warrior.

Today Ashley is riding Galahad, their young

quarter horse gelding. I watch her gallop Galahad around the arena. They look pretty fast to me. Then Mr. Harper hollers from the far side of the ring, "Go!"

Immediately Galahad takes off like he's on fire. Chunks of dirt fly behind him. I can hear his heaving breath from where Dream and I stand.

"Now! Turn it on!" Mr. Harper shouts. He's holding a giant stopwatch in one hand. He clicks it, then divides his gaze between the watch and his horse. "Stop!"

Galahad slides to a stop. Ashley shakes dust from her long blonde curls and walks Galahad over to her dad. They talk for a minute. Then I see Ashley's shoulders slump. She nods and rides Galahad to a starting position again.

If I were Ashley, I'd want to ride those horses night and day. I'd love to work with Galahad, time the runs, get Mr. Harper's instructions all to myself.

But Ashley's not me. Sometimes I think she doesn't even like to ride. Not like I do, anyway.

Ashley seems to finally see me. "Ellie! Hi!"

Mr. Harper waves. He says something to Ashley, and she walks Galahad over to meet me.

Dream and I go through the opening in the arena and stop when Dream and Galahad are nose to nose.

"You and Galahad looked great out there," I tell her. "He's so fast."

"You think so?" Ashley asks like I'd know more about it than she would. "Dad says Galahad has a long way to go."

I holler, "Hey" to Ashley's dad.

Mr. Harper walks up and pats Galahad's broad chest. The horse is barely sweating. "Hi, Ellie. Dream is looking good, kiddo. Is she still on the Omolene?"

"Yeah."

"Might want to cut back on it, with all the spring grass you've got in your backyard." He faces Dream and squints into her eyes. Then he lifts her upper lip and checks her teeth. "She's a sound horse, Ellie. You got yourself a good one."

"I know, Mr. Harper. Thanks."

He tilts his head and puts his hand under Dream's jaw. "She been feeling good?"

"Yes. I mean, I think so." My heart is starting to trot. "Why? Is there something wrong?"

"I'm sure there's not, honey." He moves his hand to Dream's chest. Then he walks back to her flank. "I'll check just to be sure, okay?"

I can't answer because my throat is too tight. If something ever happened to Dream, I don't know what I'd do.

7

Go?

"Don't look so scared, Ellie," Mr. Harper says. "I'm just making certain everything's okay." He pulls out his stopwatch and moves in front of Dream. I'm still sitting on her back, and I wonder if she can feel me shaking. "Hold her still while I check her heart rate." With his stopwatch in his left hand, he slips his right hand down the groove in Dream's neck to where it meets the chest.

I can't breathe while he counts the beats of my horse's heart. It seems like minutes pass before he takes his hand away from Dream's chest and clicks off the stopwatch.

"Looks like 35," he says.

"No!" I cry.

Ashley rides up closer. "Dad, is that good or bad?"

"It's great. Ellie, it's fine. A normal heart rate for a horse can be anywhere between 27 and 50 or so. Dream's is perfect."

"Really?" I stroke Dream's neck. "You would tell me if something was wrong. Right?"

"Of course. What do you say we check respiratory while we're at it?"

I know that means breathing. "I haven't felt her having any trouble breathing."

"Good. Move your leg up a minute, will you, Ellie?"

I curl my left leg so Mr. Harper can put his open hand on Dream's side.

Again, I can't breathe.

Without saying a word, he moves from Dream's side to her head. He bends down and studies her nostrils. I lean to the side so I can see what he's doing. I think he's watching her nostrils get wide, then relax. Wide . . . and relax. That's how he's counting her breaths.

"Got it," he says. "She's at 12 breaths per minute."

"That's not very many." Tears push at my eyes. I think I'm going to be sick.

"Ellie, that's normal," Mr. Harper says quickly. "Average respiratory rate is between 8 and 16 breaths per minute. So Dream is right in there." He strokes her blaze and straightens her forelock. "I'm sorry if I worried you."

"Why did you test Dream's heart rate in the first place, Dad?" Ashley asks.

"I'm not sure." He shrugs. "You hang around

horses as long as I have, and you get a feel for things. Sometimes you're right. Sometimes you're wrong. I'm glad I was wrong this time."

So am I.

"Are you here to practice for your race, Ellie?" Ashley asks.

In all the worry and fuss over Dream, I nearly forgot why I came out here. "Right. I thought I'd practice quick starts. Maybe get Dream used to the idea of running hard in the arena instead of practicing all the gaits like we usually do."

"That makes sense," Ashley says.

I love the Harpers' arena, where we usually have horsemanship class. It has lights and everything. Sometimes we practice here at the fairgrounds because this is where Hamilton horse shows are held. But the Harper arena is really a better surface than this one.

"So is that why you're riding here instead of

at your place?" I ask. "Because the race will be here? You know Galahad will win even if you don't practice."

When I planned this race, I guess I kind of forgot about Galahad. I was thinking Ashley would ride Cindy Lou. And Dream would have a good chance of beating her, just like I think she has a good chance of beating Larissa's three-gaited mare. Those are both American saddle horses, and they're not meant to gallop all out in a race. Galahad, on the other hand, is a quarter horse. They're the fastest horses in the world for a quarter mile.

"We're resurfacing our arena," Mr. Harper explains. "That's why Ashley couldn't ride at home. Don't worry, though. It should be set to go for horsemanship on Saturday."

"I wish I could be here for the race tomorrow," Ashley says. "Sounds like fun. But we have to leave right after school to go to the Raytown Horse Show."

"Really?" Even to myself, I sound too happy about Ashley being gone. I try again. "Really?"

Ashley grins. "Really. Good luck, Ellie." She reaches over and pats Dream on the neck. "I hope you come in first, Dream."

✯ ✯ ✯

It's turning dark by the time I get home with Dream. I check the latch again before opening the gate. There's nothing wrong with it. Maybe I'll never know how my horse got out.

Last Halloween some older kids let Cassie's pony loose. Some trick or treat that was. Maybe the same kids thought it would be funny to pull their trick on me now, even though it's not even close to October.

I lead Dream into the lean-to shelter so I can brush her, and I'm surprised to see my little brother there waiting for me.

Ethan, what's wrong?

I need you to help me with Coach.

Ethan's baseball coach isn't a bad guy. He just doesn't know what to do with Ethan, a great player who can't understand a word he says.

What did he do this time? I sign.

I don't know. That's the problem, Ellie. Before practice, he gave us this big speech. Then we played. I know I did something wrong because he kept getting mad. Then after practice, he gave us another long speech, but he talks so fast. I don't think I could have understood him even if I'd heard him with my own ears. I need to know what Coach is saying. You have to come to practice with me tomorrow.

The race is tomorrow, Ethan.

Ethan drops his hands to his sides. Then he trudges toward the house.

I run after him and tap his shoulder. *How about Saturday?*

Before the game? he signs. *And after?*

I work out a Saturday schedule in my head. If I do it right, I could be at the ball field to translate Coach's pregame pep talk. Then I could ride Dream to the Harpers' stable for horsemanship. I should be able to get back for the end of Ethan's game. And I could translate the after-game talk, no problem.

Deal, I sign.

Deal. Ethan and I shake on it.

✳ ✳ ✳

Friday morning I wake up earlier than usual. I can't wait for the race. By the end of today, everybody in Hamilton will know how great Dream is. Even Larissa. I'm going to enjoy beating her for a change.

Like I do most mornings, I get out of bed and go straight to my window. It not only faces the backyard. It *is* the backyard—or part of it, anyway. "Here, Dream!" I call.

I wait, but I don't hear the sound of her hooves. Or her morning nicker.

I whistle for her. "Come on, girl!"

Since Dream first learned to trust me enough to put her head through the window and into my room, she has done it every morning without much encouragement from me.

I stick my head out and look for her. The sun is coming up. From my bedroom, I can see the whole backyard. I survey the grounds from one end to the other and back again. No Dream.

Panic rises as I try to see into the lean-to. The

sun is still coming up, but I can see inside. Not into every corner, but almost.

She's not there. Dream is nowhere. She's gone. My horse is gone!

8

Gone

I tear out of my bedroom. What if Dream ran away? She has never run away from me. But she must have run away from someone, somewhere, before I found her.

I should have checked our fence better. I shouldn't have stopped trying to discover how my horse got out of the yard. I shouldn't have–

"Whoa!" Dad stops me in the hallway outside the bathroom. "I missed you last night. Ellie, I really need those rhymes."

"Rhymes? Dad, I–" I try to push past him.

"The rhymes for the barrel campaign? You promised you'd have a bunch of rhymes for me. I really need those before–"

"I can't talk now. Dream is gone!"

"What? What do you mean, *gone*?"

"I opened my window and called for her, but she didn't come."

Dad smiles at me. "Well, that doesn't mean she's gone."

"I looked. I couldn't see her in the yard. Not anywhere." I can't stand here talking about it. I need to go look for my horse.

I race past Dad toward the back door.

Ethan stops me. *What's the matter?*

Not now! I sign. *Dream is missing.*

Mom rushes into the kitchen. I keep going for the back door, but Ethan must have signed her up to date. She catches me at the door and opens it before I can. "When did you realize Dream was gone?" she asks. "I'll help you find her, honey."

Dad and Ethan follow us into the backyard.

And there stands Dream.

"Well, that was easier than chewing gum," Mom says. "Guess I'll be off for the cat farm." She turns to me. "Don't suppose I can count on you for quarantine cat duty?"

I'm still staring at Dream. I'm too stunned to answer her.

"Didn't think so. See you folks later."

Dad runs after her to give her a good-bye kiss.

Ethan goes over to pet Dream, but she shies away from him. That's a first. Usually she loves Ethan. He shrugs and goes back inside.

I glance at the lean-to shelter, then back at Dream. I don't see how she could have been hiding in there. I would have seen her. Wouldn't I?

"Don't ever do that again. Okay, Dream? You almost gave me a heart attack."

A lot of mornings I ride Dream before school starts. But not today. "You rest up for the big race today," I tell her. I give her a big hug. "We're going to show them who Ellie's Dream really is."

When I step away from her, my pajama top is wet. Dream must be sweaty, although I can't imagine why.

I scurry into the house and get dressed for school. The last thing I need is to get in trouble for being late. Miss Hernandez might make me stay after school. And I can't. Not today.

I have a race to win.

★ ★ ★

I make it to school on time. But it's a lousy day in class just the same. Miss Hernandez gives us a practice math test to prepare for the proficiencies. I miss half the questions.

On the way to lunch our teacher stops me. "Ellie, I thought you said you were ready for math proficiencies. Everything all right?"

It's almost worse when a teacher is nice to me when I know I don't deserve nice. "I'm sorry, Miss Hernandez. Guess I better study harder, huh?" Studying harder shouldn't be that tough since I haven't studied at all yet. I will. I just need to get the race over first.

✷ ✷ ✷

An hour after school lets out, Dream and I are lined up for the first annual Fourth-Grade Horse Race.

Colt and Bullet are standing next to us. Then Cassie on Misty, Larissa on Custer's Darling

Delight, Rashawn on Dusty, and Aiden Zeller and Kaitlyn Ferguson, both on bay mares.

I think Dream must be as excited as I am to get this race going. She paws the ground and jerks her head up and down.

Brooks, a fourth grader and one of Colt's best friends, is the official starter. "Horses to your marks!" he shouts.

"It's not auto racing, Brooks," Colt teases.

"Start your engines!" Brooks yells.

"Not funny!" Larissa whines.

"Go!"

Dream and I explode from the starting line. Most of the thundering hooves I hear are behind me. Bullet and Colt have already dropped back. Larissa must have had trouble with her high-strung horse because I can't even see her in my side vision.

For the first quarter of the arena, Rashawn

takes the lead. Dusty's strides are so long he barely has to trot to stay ahead. After that, Dusty wears out and slows to a walk.

The two bay mares are running neck and neck. They're even with Cassie and me until their riders start bumping into each other.

"Move over, Aiden!" Kaitlyn shouts.

"*You* scoot over!" Aiden shouts back.

Their squabble makes them drop back in the race.

That leaves Cassie and me in the lead coming around the curve to the home stretch. Little Misty's legs move so fast that I see a blur when I glance at them.

Dream is fast, but I think she's fading. She tosses her head and snorts. When I try to settle her down, she gets even more restless. She's acting like she's tired of racing.

We drop farther behind Cassie and Misty.

Kaitlyn's bay mare whizzes by me. Then Aiden's horse.

"First place!" Brooks yells. "The winner is . . . Cassie Bennet! And her pony, what's-its-name."

"Misty!" Cassie shouts.

Kaitlyn gallops across the finish line. "Second place!" she cries. "At least I beat Aiden."

The rest of us trail in one by one. I think Aiden comes in third, but it doesn't really matter to me. Only first place counts. The winner.

And the winner isn't Dream.

Some of the other fourth graders have come out to watch. They cheer and shout out Cassie's name. "Cassie! Cassie! Cassie!"

Colt rides up on Bullet. He's wearing a cowboy hat, and he tips it at Cassie. "Mighty fine race, Miss Cassie," he says in a lousy cowboy accent.

Cassie is laughing like it's all just a fun game to her. She does a fake bow from Misty's back.

"Thank you, thank you! But Misty is the real winner. Not little ol' me."

Larissa storms up on foot, dragging her million-dollar horse behind her. I don't even know what happened to her. "I cannot believe Phony Pony won this stupid race."

"Don't take it so hard, Larissa," Cassie says. "Who knew ponies were so fast? Hey! Maybe that's why they called it the *Pony* Express."

I laugh at her Pony Express joke. Then I congratulate Misty and Cassie. I'm really trying to be a good sport. I even tell Larissa she ran a good race. She growls something under her breath and storms off.

Everybody else thanks me for starting such a cool race. Several third graders have shown up. They claim they'll faithfully carry on the wonderful tradition of the Fourth-Grade Horse Race.

But inside, all I want to do is go home.

Dream lost the race. I wanted everybody to see how fast she is. And instead, I'm right back where I started. I am a loser. And even though Dream could never be a loser, everybody thinks she is.

9

Tricks

Once I'm home, I brush Dream and cool her off. She's sweatier than usual, so it takes me a long time. I tell her that I love her and that she did great. But I know nobody else is thinking about how great my horse is.

Pinto Cat tries to hop up onto Dream's back like she always does. But Dream shakes her off.

That's a first.

"Sorry, Pinto Cat," I say.

The calico struts away, tail high and switching like she's scolding her friend.

I muck out the yard and fertilize bushes and trees. We have the healthiest trees in town.

When I'm done, I walk the fence again, checking posts and planks. Even when I'm feeling down, I love being around my horse. I feel better simply being close to her. And I think more clearly when I talk to Dream.

I pick up a soft-bristle brush and go back to grooming Dream. Right about now in every house with a fourth grader in Hamilton, families will be talking about Cassie and Misty winning the race. The other kids will fuss over Misty at horsemanship tomorrow. And I'm glad. At least, part of me is glad. I'm happy for Misty and for Cassie. I really am. If Dream and I couldn't win that race, I'd want Cassie to.

But I can't stop wishing people were talking about Dream and how special *my* horse is.

Maybe I could teach Dream a few tricks. I read

a book once on how to get your horse to say yes and no, to count, and to bow. Stuff like that.

I'm still brushing Dream when I hear the back door slam. I expect to see my brother, but instead it's Colt.

He lifts a hand in a half wave. "Hey, Ellie."

"What's up?" I can tell something's wrong. Colt and I have been best buddies since kindergarten.

He shrugs. "Looks like your family just got bigger this weekend. I have to stay with you guys. Mom's going out of town on business. And she can't find a house sitter on short notice. She even tried Dad, but he's not answering the phone."

Since Colt's parents split up, Colt is supposed to go to his dad's in St. Louis every other weekend. But I don't think that's working out.

"Cool. You can help me teach Dream a couple of tricks." I nod for him to come over. But when he does, Dream sidesteps out of the way.

"I don't know what's gotten into Dream. She's not herself today. Don't take it personal. She just shook off Pinto Cat." I scratch Dream's withers and under her jaw. That always calms her down and can even put her to sleep. But not today. She won't hold still.

"Maybe it's a full moon," Colt says. "Weird things are happening over at our place too. Somebody—or some*thing*—must have broken into the barn really early this morning. Then whatever it was disappeared into thin air." He says this in his bad imitation of a monster's voice. "It ate more grain from the bin. I mean a lot of it, too."

I glance up at the sky. It's pretty dark. Only a sliver of the moon is filled in. "Somehow I don't think we can blame the moon, Colt."

Mom finally gets home from the cat farm and calls us in to dinner. Ethan is so psyched that Colt's staying over, he barely touches his fried chicken.

His fingers are too busy signing about the game tomorrow. Ethan says he gets to pitch.

"So, Ellie," Dad begins. He glances at Colt, then back at me. "Don't suppose you have those . . . *things* you promised me and whatnot?"

"What things, Dad?"

"You know. The *things*. Sings."

It's a bad rhyme, but good enough to remind me that I forgot to come up with a list of rhymes for Dad's barrel campaign. I guess Dad must be worried that Colt will tell his mother that I have to help with the rhyming jingles.

"Um . . . I'll get right on those *things* I *bring* that *sing* and *ring*."

Mom is in top form as dinner storyteller. "Wish you all could have been at the cat farm today. I was petting one of those poor quarantined cats"—she pauses to give me a meaningful look because that's really my job—"and this fella came in dressed to the nines. Shiny suit, ironed shirt, silk tie. 'Madam,' he says to me, 'I would like a kitten for my grand-daughter.' He glanced at his watch. '*Now*, if you please.' Well, I told him he'd need to fill out papers and have a background check like everyone else.

"'Do you have any idea who you're talking to?' he bellowed. I told him I didn't, but I wouldn't use that against his granddaughter. I've learned not to judge people by their kinfolk. That set him off on a string of words the likes of which prompted me to cover the ears of the cat I was holding.

"Long story short, I turned that bag of air down flat. Not that difficult to tell the goat from the sheep on a sunny day in Poughkeepsie. I gave him one piece of advice passed to me by your granny: Never miss a good chance to keep your mouth shut tighter than Ebenezer Scrooge."

I watch Colt's face while Mom talks. His

eyes twinkle, and the corners of his mouth can't keep from turning up. Colt told me once that my mom says more words to him in one day than his mother says in a year.

Mom leans back in her chair and groans. "I'm full as a tick on a bulldog. Anybody want dessert?"

★ ★ ★

After dinner Colt and I go out back to see if we can teach Dream a few tricks before horsemanship tomorrow. I whistle for Dream. She's standing in the back of the yard and doesn't turn around. I call out to her, "Dream! Come here, girl!"

Instead of running to me like she always does, she paces the fence and pays no attention to me.

"Okay," I tell Colt, "now I know something weird's going on. Stay here. I'll go get her."

As it turns out, it's not as easy to catch my

horse as it usually is. When I get close, she pivots and walks away. She does this four times before I can grab her halter.

"What's going on with you, girl? It's only Colt and me. Come on. You're going to learn a few tricks. It'll be fun."

I walk Dream back to Colt. He has already picked a couple of handfuls of grass for us to use as treats and rewards.

"The book said the easiest trick to teach a horse is to shake hands," I explain.

"Cool. How do you do it?"

I let Colt hold Dream's halter. Then I stand beside her, kind of like I do to clean out her front hoof, but more in front of her shoulder. "Okay. Don't let her pull backward on you."

I lean into her shoulder so she takes the weight off her left foreleg. Then I grab her knee and bend it. She lets me lift her leg, but when I try to pull it forward like a handshake, she jerks her hoof out of my hand.

"I'll try that again. I forgot to tell her to shake. I read that you need to say the words the same every time. They said most horses won't get it the first time."

I go through the same routine. Only this time I remember to say, "Shake, Dream." At least I get the leg forward and halfway up before she yanks it down again.

Six more times I give it a try. Each time I repeat, "Shake, Dream." And each time I have Colt hand me grass to reward her. But every single try, she pulls her hoof away before we really get a friendly shake. She's not even that interested in her reward. Usually Dream loves eating grass from my hand.

"Maybe this would work better with the right leg," I consider. "The book said that if you teach a horse to shake with both legs, you can work in a second trick. You can point to which leg you want to shake, and the horse will give it to you."

Colt shrugs. "Whatever you say. I'm just along for the ride."

I repeat everything from Dream's right side this time. But it's the same story. No shaking. And no grass eating.

When I call it a night and let Dream go, she bolts away. She doesn't stop until she reaches the end of the pasture. Then she paws the ground and paces the fence.

Colt and I leave the backyard in semidarkness. Above us, stars have poked through the sky. I spot the Big Dipper and Orion without even trying.

"We should have brought Bullet over," I say. "Maybe he could have learned a trick or two."

"The only trick I'm interested in is barrel racing. You think we can squeeze in time tomorrow to get going with those barrels?"

I feel a stab of guilt. We should have done that instead of wasting the night on Dream's tricks. "Definitely! We'll do it tomorrow."

★ ★ ★

The next morning I open my bedroom window and call Dream. But she doesn't come. Just like yesterday, I stare out the window and survey the backyard. I can't see Dream anywhere.

I have got to get to the bottom of this.

I pull on my jeans and T-shirt and lean out my window as far as I can without falling. "Dream! Here, girl!"

No Dream.

There's a knock on my door. I run to open it.

There stand Ethan and Colt, both rubbing their eyes and still wearing their pajamas. Cowboy pajamas—both of them. When Colt stays over, he sleeps on an air mattress in Ethan's room. One side of his face has dots on it from the little buttons on the mattress.

"What's going on?" Colt demands. "Were you trying to wake the whole neighborhood?"

That *would* be a trick since we don't have neighbors. "Dream's gone again." I sign it too so my bleary-eyed brother can see.

Not this again, Ethan signs.

I drag both of them to the backyard. On the way, I explain to Colt about Dream going missing but turning up again. I remind him that Dream had to have gotten out before she showed up in the school library.

Barefoot, we step onto dewy grass and peer into the yard.

"See?" I tell them. "My horse isn't–"

Ethan elbows me and points toward the gate. I turn in time to see my horse galloping toward us from outside the fence. She speeds up as she gets closer. Her hooves pound the wet grass. She reaches the fence and leaps.

Ellie's Dream jumps over the gate with the ease of a flying bird.

10

Jump

"Did you see that?" I need to ask Colt if that was for real because this is the kind of thing I imagine all the time. "Did you?" I demand.

"I saw it, all right. That was amazing!" Colt says. "What a jump!"

Ethan steps in front of us so he can be part of the conversation. *Ellie, that must be how Dream got out and showed up in the library! And maybe you weren't crazy after all when you thought she was out of the yard.*

I flip my fingers from my chin in the *thank you* sign and hope Ethan picks up on the sarcasm.

"She really did it," I mutter. "My horse is a jumper. *That's* her trick. Jumping!" I turn to Colt. "We have to get Mr. Harper to set up jumps at his arena today."

Colt has his arms folded like he's cold. "You want to get Dream to jump at horsemanship practice?"

"I've never wanted anything more in my whole life. Except when I wanted a horse and didn't have one," I add.

⚝ ⚝ ⚝

An hour later Colt and I are at the Harpers' arena. We gulped down breakfast, then rode Bullet and Dream straight here.

"Thank you for doing this, Mr. Harper." From my spot on Dream's back, I watch as he and Colt set up jumps across the arena. I'd help, but I'm looking after Bullet and Dream.

"Thank *you*, Ellie," Mr. Harper says. He sets down a big wooden X, walks two steps, and places another one. Then he sets a lightweight bar across the two wooden Xs. "I have been trying to get Ashley to work on jumps with Warrior. Should be fun for all of us. I'll keep the jumps low."

"Not too low," I say. "Maybe you could set up one high jump. We could see how things are working out and try it if it's going well." I know Dream and I will want to try.

Dream paws the ground. She sidesteps, dancing side to side.

"Take it easy, girl," I whisper. "I'm as anxious as you are to get at those jumps. Just wait until they see you sail over the highest bar. Then everybody will get it. They'll see for themselves how great you really are."

Ellie and Dream line up for the American
Royal jumping competition. Crowds have
gathered from all across the state of Missouri.
And some from Kansas and Iowa too. Dream
paws the ground. Then they're off. Ellie
and Dream take the first jump as if it's not
there. Dream clears the second jump and
the third. She turns to try the giant fence
jump, which no horse has ever attempted
before. Especially not Custer's Darling
Delight. Dream's hooves strike the ground
hard. Ellie James clings to her pinto. They
lift up, up, up . . . and over! The crowd sits
in stunned silence. Then everyone breaks
into thunderous applause. "Ellie! Ellie!
Dream! Dream!"

I stop daydreaming because Dream is getting edgy. She won't stand still, and I'm trying to hold Bullet's reins while Colt sets up the jumps. I dismount and lead Bullet to the hitching post. "There you go, guy. Colt will be right back."

No way will Dream settle for being hitched to a post today, so I keep her moving. We trot around the Harpers' stables. It's a perfect-weather day. If I had the power to make it hotter or colder, I wouldn't know which way to go.

Harpers' doesn't smell like K. C. Stables, where Larissa boards her horse. Here, there's still a barn smell, earthy and horsey. Fancy stables like K. C. Stables take all the horse smell out. If I had to put Dream in a stable—and I'd never want that to happen—this is where I'd come.

Larissa is last to arrive. A trailer backs up to the arena, and the driver gets out. He reminds me of Frosty the Snowman, all middle and almost no legs. He waddles around to the back of the trailer and lets down the ramp. Then he backs Custer down and out of the trailer.

Larissa's lanky three-gaited gelding is gorgeous, all right. But he reminds me of runway models on TV. They look pretty and all, but you'd never want one of them for your mom or your best friend.

"I still can't believe you couldn't get me here on time!" Larissa whines. "I'm telling Daddy you made me late."

The driver has his back to Larissa and his front to me. He rolls his eyes. "Sorry, miss. If I'd known those trucks planned to have an accident on Highway 36, I would have taken an alternate route. Plus, we had ball game traffic."

Ball game! I forgot all about Ethan's game today. And I promised I'd be there to sign Coach's pregame talk. Why didn't Ethan remind me?

But I know the answer to that question. Ethan didn't want to bother me. He never does. He doesn't ask for much. I should have come through for him on this one thing.

I determine to get to the ballpark before the game ends so I can at least sign Coach's after-game talk to the boys.

Larissa had better not make us all late.

The driver of the K. C. Stables trailer snaps a leather lead rope on Custer and hands it to Larissa. Then he disappears inside the trailer cab and comes out with an English saddle, a blanket, and a bridle, plus another bag. After he hangs the saddle and blanket and bridle over the fence and drops the bag, he heads back to the trailer.

"Where do you think you're going?" Larissa demands. "You don't expect me to saddle my own horse, do you?"

"We can get it, Larissa," Mr. Harper calls. He flashes a smile at the driver.

"No thank you," she replies. "That's what we pay these people for." She holds out the lead rope for the driver to take.

Colt jogs over from the jumps and takes the reins. He holds Custer while the driver saddles Larissa's horse without a word.

Mr. Harper gives Rashawn and me English saddles to use. I saddle Dream, then stand back and admire how awesome she looks in the neat leather saddle.

I glance at Dusty. Her saddle looks like a wallet on an elephant.

Rashawn catches me staring. "High fashion, don't you think?" Then she bursts out laughing. She's already having fun. Sometimes I think that girl could have a good time taking math proficiencies.

I block out every thought of proficiencies and homework. No way am I going to let math ruin Dream's big moment.

Finally we're all set. Everybody falls into line so we can take turns jumping. I let Cassie, Rashawn, and Colt in ahead of me. Larissa pushes in behind Ashley.

Mr. Harper gives us all some tips about jumping before having Ashley demonstrate. "Any horse can be a jumper," he begins. "Doesn't matter what breed or bloodline. The only requirement is that your horse loves to jump. And you never know that until you try. Some horses bred for jumping never develop the passion for it. Other horses come by a jumping talent naturally and only need to be nurtured."

"That's how it is with Dream," I tell Colt.

Larissa turns in her saddle. "Ellie, don't tell me you actually think your little spotted pony could be a jumper?" She laughs, but it sounds like a blue jay robbing a robin's nest. That's what my granny would have said.

"She'll see," I whisper to Dream. "They'll all see." I reach down to stroke her neck. My hand comes back wet. Dream is already sweating foam as if we've been racing all morning. But I haven't done anything except walk her. And it's not that hot out.

Mr. Harper is explaining the jumps he and Colt have set up. "These are all simple cavalletti jumps. I wouldn't let any of you do this if I didn't know you're ready. I've worked with most of you for a couple of years now. Take it slow. Practice holding the reins with a handful of mane. Remember the two-point position I taught you. Let your horse take your weight out of the saddle. Put your weight into your stirrups. Let your knees keep you steady. And keep your helmets on."

I haven't paid much attention to the jumps, so I take a good look now. The sides look like big white Xs. The pole rests right on them. Each jump is set a little higher than the one before it. The last jump, farther down and off the course, is really high.

"Ashley," Mr. Harper says, "take Warrior through the regular jumps to demonstrate."

Warrior goes straight over each jump with no mistakes. But Ashley steers her horse away from the high fence at the end. She doesn't even attempt it.

Rashawn goes next because Mr. Harper calls her up ahead of Larissa. But Dusty isn't into it. She steps over the first two jumps and walks straight through the next two. Rashawn laughs and pets her horse's neck as if Dusty won a trophy.

Cassie and Misty give the jumps a good try. Misty heaves himself over the first jump. We cheer. But the pony's legs are too short for the other jumps.

"My turn!" Larissa cries, heading for the starting line.

"Ellie!" Mr. Harper calls like he hasn't heard Larissa. "It's your turn. Ride Dream up here."

I urge Dream forward. Instead of walking on, she paws the ground. Faster and harder, she paws. Dirt flies up. I feel her tremble. I'm trembling too. Something is wrong. Dream stops pawing. Her neck cranes around. She stares at her stomach like it's not even part of her body.

I jump off and stand in front of her. "Mr. Harper, something's wrong with Dream!"

11

Help!

"Please! Help!" I'm shaking. I keep my eyes on my horse, but everything looks blurry through the tears. Her motions are jerky. She wheels her neck around so fast her nose bumps her belly.

I want to take off the saddle. Maybe that's what's bothering her. I step toward my horse but feel a firm hand on my shoulder, pulling me back.

"Don't, Ellie. Don't get any closer. Dream is in pain. She might not know what she's doing."

"In pain?" The thought of my horse being in

pain makes me feel like I'm going to throw up. "What's wrong with her? What happened?"

Mr. Harper tosses his cell phone to Ashley. "Call the vet. Doc Snyder is in my contacts."

"Tell me what's wrong with Dream!" I cry. My chest hurts. It's hard to catch my breath.

Colt takes hold of my arm like he's afraid I'm going to faint. "Mr. Harper, what's wrong with Ellie's horse? She was okay this morning."

"Are you sure?" He looks from Colt to me. "Has Dream been acting . . . strange in any way lately?"

"No," Colt answers.

But I'm not so sure. "Maybe." I picture Dream in the library.

"How? What's been different about her?" Mr. Harper hangs on to Dream's reins. I don't know when he took them from me.

"She jumped our fence and came to school and—"

100

He interrupts me. "I know. Ashley told me. What else? Little things, Ellie. Think."

I close my eyes, then open them as images of Dream come back—pictures I must have shoved to the back of my brain. "She *has* been acting funny. Dream always comes when I call her. But for the last couple of days, she hasn't. And she walked away from me when I came out to catch her."

Mr. Harper nods and waits for more.

"She shied away from Ethan, and she likes Ethan."

"She did the same thing with me," Colt adds.

"And she's been sweating too much. She paws the ground a lot." I glance at my horse and realize she's doing it right now.

"She keeps looking at her stomach." Mr. Harper's face is filled with worry wrinkles.

"I know! Why? What is it?" I demand.

"I'm not a vet, but I'm pretty sure Dream has colic."

I'm not exactly sure what colic is, but I've heard of horses dying from it. I can't ask anything more. I'm crying too hard.

"What's colic?" Colt asks for me.

"It's a stomachache," Mr. Harper says. "There are lots of kinds of colic—lots of reasons for it. Dream could have gotten some water she wasn't used to. She might have eaten something she shouldn't have. There are—"

"Dad! I got the vet." Ashley runs up to us. "Doc says to keep Dream on her feet. We're supposed to walk her until she gets there." Ashley looks at me, and I can tell she's been crying too. "Ellie, Doc Snyder said you should walk Dream back to your place. She'll meet you there."

The other kids have gathered around us. They shout good luck and other encouragement as we lead Dream away. I hear Cassie's voice and Rashawn's, but I don't know what they're saying. My heart is thumping too loud in my ears. My stomach hurts.

Mr. Harper insists on leading Dream all the way to my house. Colt walks Bullet a safe distance in front of us. I keep up with Mr. Harper. No one says a word.

Except inside, my heart and soul are talking to God. And I'm begging God not to let my horse die.

12

Waiting

The whole walk to my house, I try not to cry. Dream is the one in pain, not me. But my stomach feels upset enough that I might as well have colic too.

Mr. Harper tries to keep Dream walking, but it isn't easy. She dances and sidesteps one minute. Then the next minute she stops—just puts on the brakes. Twice she tries to lie down in the middle of the road. But Mr. Harper jerks the rope up and won't let her.

All I hear is the clip-clip, clop-clop of Dream's

hooves. And each hoof beat shouts to me, *It's all your fault. It's all your fault.*

Bullet picks up on Dream's nervousness. Colt has to turn him in little circles to calm him down.

Finally we turn onto my road.

"Looks like Doc beat us here." Mr. Harper points to an old white pickup truck parked in front of my house.

The truck door opens, and a girl with long, curly brown hair hops out. She looks like she could be in high school. She's wearing cowboy boots, skinny jeans, and a pink T-shirt. I study her as she walks to the back of the truck and takes out a black bag.

"Whoa!" Colt mutters. "*That's* the veterinarian?"

"She's young, but she's good," Mr. Harper says. "Best vet we've ever had around here." He waves to her. "Hey, Doc. Thanks for coming out so fast."

"Glad to, John. Let's get this mare settled so I can take a look at her."

Mr. Harper introduces Colt and me to the vet. Colt shakes her hand and says something about how great it is that she's a vet.

"Can you help Dream? She's in pain. Her stomach . . ." Tears make my voice sound like I'm underwater. "Dream is such a good horse. She really is. She would never hurt anybody. Please?"

The vet shifts her bag to one hand and puts her other hand on my shoulder. "I promise I'll do everything I can for your horse, Ellie."

I nod . . . and pray that's enough.

We get Dream into the lean-to. I've already cleaned it, but I sprinkle more straw on the floor. Dr. Snyder ties my horse on a short lead so she can't lie down. Then she listens to Dream's belly and takes her temperature.

Mr. Harper fills Dr. Snyder in on the details

about Dream. He describes my horse's symptoms. He tells her what we did for Dream and how she acted on the walk over here.

A horn honks. Ashley and her mother drive up.

"I wish I could stay, Ellie," Mr. Harper says. "Will you be okay? When will your folks get home?"

I can't think straight. Where *are* my parents?

Then I remember. "Mom's at the cat farm outside of town." It's where I should have been. Would it have made a difference if I'd gone there? What if I'd done what I was supposed to do? What if I'd hung out with the quarantined cats instead of making Dream race and jump?

"I think your dad's home," Colt says to me. "His car is in the driveway. I'll go see, okay?" He doesn't wait for an answer. Colt slips off Bullet's bridle and lets him graze. Then he takes off for the house.

Ashley comes to the back fence and leans over. "Is Dream okay?"

"Doc Snyder will take care of her, honey," Mr. Harper answers.

Colt comes outside with my dad. Dad's face and clothes are wrinkly on one side, like he's been napping on the couch. I run to him and let him wrap his arms around me. He strokes my hair like he used to when I was little.

"Colt told me what's going on," Dad says. "Thanks for coming, Doc Snyder." He shakes her hand. Then he turns to Mr. Harper. "John, thank you. Appreciate what you did for Ellie and whatnot. You go on. We'll take it from here. Thanks again."

Things are happening all around me—people are talking and pointing and shaking hands. I'm in the middle of it, but it doesn't feel real. Nothing feels real except the fact that my horse is sick. Very sick.

"Ellie," Dr. Snyder calls from the far side of the lean-to. "Can you come help me, please? I think Dream will be calmer if you'll come around and talk to her."

Doc guides me to stand by Dream's muzzle. I watch my horse's nostrils flare out and in, out and in. Her eyes are too wide. There's too much white. It's like she doesn't even see me.

"Will she be okay?" I ask. "Tell me she'll be all right."

"I need to find out how bad her colic is." Dr. Snyder runs her hand along Dream's side. When she gets to the belly, Dream's ears flatten back.

"Look out!" I shout.

Dream whips her head around and shows her teeth . . . like she means to bite.

13

My Fault

"Dream has never bitten anyone," I tell Dr. Snyder. "Ever. She's a sweet horse."

Doc Snyder doesn't seem angry. She goes back to scratching Dream's withers. "You hurt, don't you, girl?" she murmurs to Dream. "It's okay. I understand."

When Doc turns to me this time, she looks serious. "Ellie, we need to figure out if something Dream ate might be giving her colic. I'd like to know what caused this bellyache so I can help get rid of it."

Colt eases through the lean-to and stands beside me. "Is colic . . . is it serious?"

"It can be. That's why it would help if we knew the cause. Understand?"

We both nod.

"Good. Mr. Harper told me you said that your horse has been acting different lately. Tell me about that."

I tell her everything I can think of—how Dream has been restless, how she's taken to pawing the ground for no reason, how she sidesteps like she's nervous, how she's been hard to catch and skittish lately.

She nods and waits for more.

I try, but I can't think of anything else.

"Do you know if your water is good?" she asks.

This time Dad answers. He has inched toward the corner of the lean-to a few feet from us. "The water's fresh. It's the same as what we use in the house, and it moves through the tank constantly."

"How about the hay? Was it musty when you bought it? Did it smell funny?"

We shake our heads. It smelled like hay.

Dr. Snyder keeps guessing. "Is there anything in this pasture—your yard—that the mare might have gotten hold of and eaten?"

"No way," I answer. "I walk the yard every night to make sure. There's nothing here but grass." Then I think of something. "Dream did jump the fence and get out a couple of times."

Dr. Snyder puts her hand on mine. "This is important, Ellie. When did she get out? Where did she go? She might have gotten into something that—"

"That's it!" Colt exclaims. "Ellie, remember? I told you something's been into our grain bin. At least twice. It must have been Dream! I'll bet she broke out of your yard and came to our barn and got into the oats."

Now my head really is spinning. "But your oats can't be bad. Bullet isn't sick."

"How much grain did she eat, Colt?" Doc asks.

"A whole lot," he answers. "We keep the oats in a big rubber trash bin about this high." He raises his arm to show her. "She just about emptied the thing."

"What can we do?" I don't know if I'm relieved that we know what's wrong, or even more worried.

Dad strokes Dream's sweaty neck, even though I know he's afraid of my horse—and all horses, for that matter. "Won't she just vomit if she overeats?"

I know the answer to Dad's question. But I wait for the vet to explain.

"Horses can't vomit, Mr. James. As a vet, I wish they could. Other animals can get rid of bad things they eat, but not horses. And unfortunately horses don't have a shutoff valve on their appetites. A horse will keep eating until someone stops it. Let me walk the mare around a little bit so I can tell where she's hurting." She unties Dream and takes her out of the lean-to and into the yard.

Dad, Colt, and I watch in silence. I beg God to cure my horse. But it feels like my words float up toward the sky, then plunk back down again.

The back door slams and Ethan comes running out. I can't take my eyes off my horse to see what my brother is signing. But I can hear Colt and Dad.

"Dream's sick, Ethan," Dad explains. "It's colic. A stomachache. She ate too many oats when she got out of the fence. I should have built it higher when we knew she was getting out. I was so worried about the Harvey's Hardware account and the barrel campaign, I guess I didn't want to take the time to make more fence out here."

The barrel account! How could I have forgotten? Dad's presentation was this morning. He had to go ahead without my rhymes, without the list of words I promised him.

I can't even look at my dad. Guilt tightens around me like a burning belt.

"Mr. James," Colt says, "your fence is taller than ours. We should have gotten a real storage bin instead of that trash can. And I should have figured out what was going on with the missing oats, but all I've been thinking about lately is getting Bullet ready for barrel racing."

There's one more thing I forgot about. I let Colt *and* Bullet down.

Dad and Colt can talk all day about things they should or shouldn't have done, but it doesn't matter. I know whose fault this is. And so does God. It's not just that I didn't pick up on the warning signs of colic and how weird Dream was acting. It's not just that I didn't keep looking for an answer to how Dream was getting out or where she was going.

It's everything I haven't been doing. I was so set on proving to everybody how great my horse is that I let everything else go. I didn't just let Dream down. I let everybody down.

"So how was your game, Ethan?" Colt asks.

This time I wheel around to see my brother's answer.

We won. But I think Coach was mad at me about something. He yelled a lot in our after-game talk. And he pointed right at me. Only don't ask me why he was so fired up.

Chalk up one more letdown by Ellie James.

No wonder God doesn't answer my prayers for Dream. I don't deserve to have anyone listen to me. Especially God.

Dr. Snyder leads Dream back to us. She's

holding the lead rope high like she's trying to keep my horse on her feet.

Again I ask God to make my horse well. But I can tell by Dream's wide eyes and heavy breathing that she's still hurting.

"Well, I don't think her intestines are twisted," Doc Snyder says. "Beyond that, I'm just not sure. I'll give her a shot of butraphol to ease the pain. Then all we can do is wait and see. If the colic is mild, it should pass in twenty-four hours."

She doesn't say what will happen if the colic isn't mild. But she doesn't have to . . . because we all know.

14

P-R-A-Y-I-N-G

Ethan walks up beside me. I don't turn around. I can't face him. He touches my arm, and I feel his fingertip spelling out a word on my skin. I don't think he's ever done this before. It feels like whispering. I make out *p-r-a-y-i-n-g*. *Praying*.

I touch his hand and nod. I'm praying too. But Ethan is better at it.

I circle my fist over my heart, making the sign for *sorry*, then look in his direction.

Ethan signs, *What?* and acts like he doesn't know what I mean.

Coach's talk.

Ethan brushes it off like he's forgotten I promised to help him. Maybe he has.

But I know God hasn't.

Dr. Snyder gives Dream a shot. Dream doesn't jerk away like I do when I get shots. It's like she doesn't even feel the needle.

"You call me if she gets worse. Okay, Ellie?" Doc drops the syringe into a little metal case, then puts it into her black bag. "And try not to worry."

"Thank you," I mutter. But I don't know why grown-ups bother telling you not to worry. It doesn't do any good.

Mom finally gets back from the cat farm and finds us all in the backyard. She tells me the same thing Doc Snyder did. I should try not to worry. Only she says this in her own way. "Worry is like shoveling manure with a toothpick. Waste of time, and nobody comes out smelling like roses."

I nod.

"Come on now," Mom urges. "What we need is food. Can't expect an army to war on empty stomachs."

Everybody shuffles off toward the house. Except me.

"Ellie, I brought home sweet-and-sour pork—your favorite. And enough egg rolls to build the Great Wall of China."

I shake my head. I'm not hungry. Actually, even the thought of my favorite Chinese food makes me want to hurl. And that reminds me that Dream *can't* throw up. She has to keep everything bad inside of her.

While they're all inside eating dinner, I stay in the lean-to and talk to my horse. I'm not sure if she knows I'm here with her or not.

"I'm so sorry you have a stomachache, Dream. I wish I could do something to make it better. I'm praying. But I've done so many rotten, selfish things lately. I don't know what good my prayers are going to do you. I didn't mean to let you down. Or everybody else, either. I just wanted people to see you like I see you. You're the best horse in the whole world. So you have to get better. Okay? Please get better, Dream. Please? I can't lose you."

I stop talking because I'm choking on my words. I swipe my eyes with the back of my arm.

Colt and Ethan come back out after they've eaten. They sit with Dream and me for a long time. But I guess they don't know what to say any more than I do. They don't even talk to each other.

A little later Mom comes out and tells us a story about Granny and a sick coyote she rescued when she was a little girl. It must be a funny story because Ethan and Colt laugh. But I don't hear much of it. I'm listening to Dream's scratchy breath. It sounds like sleet landing on a plastic bag.

Dad comes out a few times. He pats Dream's head, reaching from as far away as possible. "There's a good horse," he says. "You get all that colic and whatnot out of you."

Dad strokes Dream's white blaze for several minutes, murmuring to her. He doesn't even mention the barrel campaign or how his big presentation went.

I don't ask. I can't even look my dad in the eyes.

Then he goes back in, leaving Ethan and Colt and me sitting around in silence. Pinto Cat curls up next to Ethan, but she doesn't purr.

After a while, Mom and Dad come and get Ethan for bed. Mom says Colt and I can stay a little longer.

"Anybody want a sweatshirt?" Mom asks. "It's getting *chilly con carne* out here."

I hadn't noticed. But when she mentions it, I shiver.

It seems like only a couple of minutes have passed when Mom calls from the back door, "Time for bed!"

"I can't leave Dream," I tell Colt. Tears spring into my eyes. "You have to tell Mom I need to stay with my horse."

Colt gets to his feet. He stamps one foot like it's gone to sleep. "Ellie, there's nothing you can do out here."

Pinto Cat must agree with him. The calico struts out of the lean-to and disappears deep into the yard.

"There *is* something I can do. I can stay with Dream. It's not much. But I can at least be here with my horse." The moon leaks through tiny cracks in the wood, making stripes across Colt's shirt. "I can't leave Dream. You wouldn't leave Bullet."

He stares at me, and I think I see shiny tears in

the corners of his eyes. "I get it. I'll tell your mom." He starts to go. Then he stops. When he turns around, his whole face is lit by shiny moonlight. "And I'll pray."

Then he turns and runs into the house.

Did Colt just say he'd pray?

Colt Stevens doesn't even like it when I talk to him about God. But he said he'll pray. He'll pray for Dream.

15

God's Lap

Mom tries calling me in to bed again. But I can't go.

"Please, Mom?" I shout. "You know I wouldn't sleep anyway."

She shouts back some Granny quotes about sleep and clouds and brain food. But finally she gives up and goes inside.

Minutes later Mom brings me a sleeping bag and a peanut butter sandwich. And two kisses— one for Dream, the other for the top of my head.

Dad comes out later with a blanket and a

pillow. He's in his striped pajamas. He kisses me good night and tells me to stay safe. I know he means I shouldn't get too close to Dream. I promise him.

I roll out the sleeping bag and lie on top of it. From where I am inside the lean-to, I have a clear shot of our house. Golden light spills from the windows and into the backyard. Shadows of my family move around inside. It looks like another world, like a TV show I'm watching.

I've let down every single person in that house. I wouldn't blame any of them if they didn't care what happened to me or to Dream.

The night gets darker. I pull the blanket over me and listen to Dream's breathing. It's heavy, but I think it might be getting more regular. I hope so.

Out and in. Out and in. Out and in.

I refuse to let myself sleep, but I do close my eyes. I need to talk to God. My mind moves somewhere between praying and talking. It zigzags between thinking and dreaming.

And imagining.

Just like I do lots of nights when I can't sleep or when I need to do more than the "God bless" kind of prayer, I imagine crawling onto God's lap.

I climb up onto God's lap. It's surprisingly easy to get here. It takes no effort at all, like sledding down a hill or floating downstream. I snuggle in and get comfortable. Then I open my mouth and let the words pour out. "Father, I know I don't deserve to have You listen to me."

"Why?" God asks.

"You know. We both know You know everything. You've seen everything I did all week. And worse, You saw what I should have done and didn't do. I'm sorry about not coming up with rhymes for my dad like I said I would.

And I'm sorry Mom had to do my job with the quarantined cats at the farm. I know she's got her own work to do there. And at the worm ranch. And the regular animal shelter. I really did mean to help Colt with Bullet. And to sign the talks at Ethan's game. But I didn't do any of that. Plus, I haven't even thought about doing math homework or studying for proficiencies like I promised Miss Hernandez."

I take a breath and feel the freshness of getting all that bad stuff out. It feels so good to talk things over with God. I lean my head on God's shoulder. "Please help my horse even though I've been such a rotten person all week."

I still don't open my eyes, but I'm not imagining any longer. I'm thinking. Hard. And one thing I'm thinking is that I wish Dream could get all the bad out of her like I do when I talk things over with God.

The next thing I think hard about is how much I love my horse. I don't care if she never wins a race. I don't care if she never learns a single trick or jumps a jump. I just love her. I love her because she's Dream.

I'm starting to get goose bumps, and it's not because it's cold out here. It's because something inside of me is telling me to pay attention. *I love Dream because she's Dream.*

And isn't that how God loves me? God isn't on my side because I do stuff I'm supposed to. God loves me because I'm me. Ellie.

What a stupidhead I've been to think for one second that God wouldn't answer my prayers because I messed up. I mess up all the time. I know when God does answer prayers it's sure not because I'm such a perfect kid.

God answers prayers because God is God. And Jesus already took care of my mess-ups.

I drift off to the sweet sound of crickets. Their regular chirping is like music. And the lyrics are from God: *I love you, Ellie. I love you, Ellie. I love you because you're you, Ellie.*

When I do open my eyes, I realize I must have been asleep for real. Things have changed in this lean-to.

On one side of me, Mom is lying curled up next to Dad. She's snoring. Dad is mumbling in his sleep. They're both tugging on the blanket they've brought out here.

But that's not all. On the other side of me is Ethan. Wrapped up in a baseball blanket, my brother is smiling in his sleep. And at my feet is Colt, all tucked inside Ethan's sleeping bag.

I let every one of them down, but they're here anyway. Just like God.

Without closing my eyes this time, I imagine myself on God's lap. I stretch out my hand to

Mom, Dad, Ethan, and Colt. God and I help them climb up too.

That's when I hear it. A nicker. The best sound in the whole world. A soft, rumbling sound that would be a purr if it came from a cat. Pinto Cat hears it too. She bounds from out of nowhere and leaps onto Dream's back.

I jump to my feet and nearly trip over Mom and Dad. I stumble to my horse. "Dream? Dream!"

She nickers again.

I hug her. She's not sweaty. She's not pawing the ground. She dips her muzzle into her trough and comes out with a mouthful of hay.

"You're okay!" I fire up a prayer of thanks to God. I imagine hugging my heavenly Father around the neck while Dream jumps into God's lap with the rest of us.

"Is she really okay?" Colt is standing beside

me. He strokes Dream's neck. "She's not sweaty anymore."

Mom and Dad and Ethan join us. We all stand around my horse. Somehow we're managing to laugh and cry at the same time.

When I can force myself to take my gaze from Dream, I glance around at my parents, Ethan, and Colt. They look as happy as I feel inside.

"I can't believe you guys would come out here with me—especially after the way I let you down."

"What are you talking about?" Dad asks.

"Your rhymes, Dad. I'm sorry I didn't come through for you and get you *barrel* rhymes like I said I would."

"Ellie, those jingles and slogans are *my* responsibility—not yours. Besides, it all worked out. I had to go rhyme-less. And as it happens, Harvey of Harvey's Hardware hates rhymes. He loved my plain ol' slogans about old-fashioned barrels."

I look to Mom, and she's grinning at me. "Well, I admit I could have used you at the cat farm. It's been a crazy week. But what's that got to do with the price of tulips in Greenland? We're here with you in this backyard of ours because we're family, Ellie." She elbows Colt. "And that goes for Colt here too."

Suddenly I burst into a laugh so hard Dream looks worried about *me*.

"What?" Colt asks. "What's so funny?"

I shake my head. "You guys."

What's so funny about us? Ethan signs.

"Nothing at all," I answer. "I was just wondering what Larissa will say when she hears about this."

"Hears about what?" Colt asks.

"That Ellie James doesn't just have a backyard horse." I glance around at these people who have stuck it out with me through the worst day of my life.

"I have a backyard family."

We know how much God loves us, and
we have put our trust in his love.

1 John 4:16

Horse Talk!

Bay–A reddish-brown color for a horse. A bay horse usually has a black mane and tail.

Blaze–A facial marking on a horse (usually a wide, jagged white stripe).

Canter–A horse's slow gallop; a more controlled three-beat gait.

Cutting horse–A horse (usually a quarter horse) bred to separate cows from a herd. Some cutting horses also cut around barrels in barrel racing or compete in Western horse show classes and events.

English–A style of horseback riding that is often considered more formal and classic than Western style. Riders generally sit on a flat saddle, post (rise from the saddle) on a trot, and hold the reins in both hands.

Farrier–Someone trained to care for a horse's hooves. Farriers trim hooves and put shoes on horses, but many also treat leg and tendon problems.

Flanks–The indented part of a horse's body between the ribs and the hip. Flanks may be tender to the touch.

Foreleg–One of a horse's front legs.

Forelock–The piece of hair that falls onto a horse's forehead.

Gait–The way a horse moves, as in a walk, a trot, a canter, or a gallop.

Gallop–A horse's natural and fast running gait. It's speedier than a lope or a canter.

Gelding–A male horse that has had surgery so he can't mate and produce foals (baby horses). Geldings often make the calmest riding horses.

Habit–An outfit for horseback riding or showing, usually including some kind of tailored jacket and hat.

Halter–The basic headgear worn by a horse so the handler can lead the animal with a rope.

Hand–The unit for measuring a horse's height from the withers (area between the shoulders) to the ground. One hand equals four inches (about the width of an average cowboy's hand).

Hindquarters–The back end of a horse, where much of a horse's power comes from.

Hoof pick–A hooked tool, usually made of metal, for cleaning packed dirt, stones, and gunk from the underside of a horse's hoof.

Hunter–A horse that's bred to carry a rider over jumps. In a horse show, hunters are judged on jumping ability and style.

Lead rope–A length of rope with a metal snap that attaches to a horse's halter.

Lope–The Western term for *canter*. The lope is usually smooth and slower than the canter of a horse ridden English.

Mare–A female horse over the age of four, or any female horse that has given birth.

Muzzle–The soft portion of a horse's nose between the nostrils and the upper lip.

Nicker–A soft, friendly sound made by horses, usually to greet other horses or trusted humans.

Palomino–A horse that is cream or yellow-gold in color. Palominos may be found in a number of breeds, such as the quarter horse. Even backyard horses may be palominos.

Pinto–Any horse with patches or spots of white and another color, usually brown or black.

Post–To rise up and ease back down in the saddle when the horse is at a trot. This makes the gait more comfortable for the rider. English-style riders generally post at every step.

Quarter horse–An American horse breed named because it's the fastest horse for a quarter-mile distance. Quarter horses are strong and are often used for ranch work. They're good-natured and easygoing.

Quirt–A Western-style crop, or whip, with a short handle.

Saddle bags–Bags or pouches that balance across the back of a saddle and are used to carry supplies.

Saddle horse–A saddle horse could be any horse trained to ride with a saddle. More specifically, the American saddlebred horse is an elegant breed of horse used as three- and five-gaited riding horses.

Shetland pony–A small breed, no bigger than 10.2 hands, that comes from the Shetland Islands off Scotland. Shetland ponies are the ideal size for small children, but the breed is known to be stubborn and hard to handle.

Sorrel–A horse with a reddish-brown or reddish-gold coat.

Stallion–A male horse that hasn't had surgery to prevent him from mating and producing foals.

Swayback–A sagging back on a horse, or a horse with a deeply dipped back. Being swayback is often a sign of old age in a horse.

Three-gaited–Used to describe an American saddlebred horse that has been trained to perform at a walk, trot, and canter.

Throatlatch–The strap part of the bridle that helps keep the bridle on. It goes under a horse's throat, running from the right ear and loosely fastening below the left ear.

Trot–The two-beat gait where a horse's legs move in diagonal pairs. A trot is generally a choppy ride.

Western–A style of horseback riding used by cowboys in the American West. Western horseback riders usually use heavier saddles with saddle horns and hold both reins in one hand.

Whicker–A low sound made by a horse. A whicker is sometimes thought to be a cross between a whinny and a nicker.

Whinny–A horse's neigh, or to make a neighing sound. A whinny may be a horse's call to another horse or a cry of alarm.

Whorl–A twist of hair that grows in the opposite direction from the surrounding coat. This patch is usually on a horse's forehead.

Withers–The top of a horse's shoulders, between the back and the neck. The height of a horse is measured from the withers to the ground.

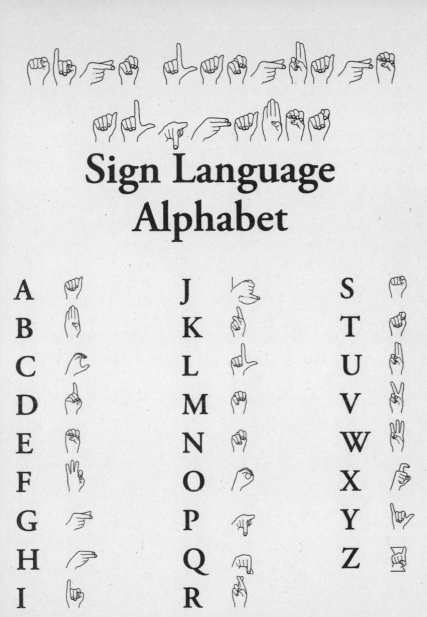

Sign Language Alphabet

A

B

C

D

E

F

G

H

I

J

K

L

M

N

O

P

Q

R

S

T

U

V

W

X

Y

Z

About the Author

Dandi Daley Mackall grew up riding horses, taking her first solo bareback ride when she was three. Her best friends were Sugar, a pinto; Misty, probably a Morgan; and Towaco, an Appaloosa. Dandi and her husband, Joe; daughters, Jen and Katy; and son, Dan (when forced), enjoy riding Cheyenne, their paint. Dandi has written books for all ages, including Little Blessings books, *Degrees of Guilt: Kyra's Story*, *Degrees of Betrayal: Sierra's Story*, *Love Rules*, *Maggie's Story*, the Starlight Animal Rescue series, and the bestselling Winnie the Horse Gentler series. Her books (about 450 titles) have sold more than 4 million copies. She writes and rides from rural Ohio.

Visit Dandi at www.dandibooks.com.